Postman Pat
and the
Letter-Puzzle

Story by **John Cunliffe**   Pictures by **Joan Hickson**
From the original Television designs by **Ivor Wood**

Hippo

Scholastic Children's Books,
Scholastic Publications Ltd,
7-9 Pratt Street, London NW1 0AE, UK

Scholastic Inc.,
730 Broadway, New York, NY 10003, USA

Scholastic Canada Ltd,
123 Newkirk Road, Richmond Hill,
Ontario, Canada L4C 3G5

Ashton Scholastic Pty Ltd,
PO Box 579, Gosford, New South Wales,
Australia

Ashton Scholastic Ltd,
Private Bag 1, Penrose, Auckland,
New Zealand

First published in the UK by Scholastic Publications Ltd, 1989
This edition published 1993
Text copyright © John Cunliffe 1989 and 1993
Illustrations copyright © Scholastic Publications Ltd and Woodland
Animations Limited, 1989

A longer version of this story has been previously published as
a Handy Hippo

ISBN: 0 590 54141 2

10 9 8 7 6 5 4 3 2 1

Printed in Hong Kong by Paramount Printing Group Ltd.

"Just look at those leaves," said Pat.
"Turning brown already. We'll soon be
thinking of Christmas."

Pat was on his way with his letters. Jess
was in his basket at Pat's side. He wasn't
thinking of Christmas. He was thinking of
rabbits. He had just seen two fat ones,
running across the school field.

When Pat arrived at Greendale Farm, Katy said, "Guess what we've got!"

"...a pony," said Tom. "Come and see it!"

"All right," said Pat. "But I mustn't stay long. I have such a lot of letters today."

Pat put his bag of letters down, next to baby Paul, and went to see the pony.

The pony trotted across the field to them,
and they gave it an apple. Pat stroked it.
"She's a real beauty," said Pat.

Just as they were all going back into the house, they could hear Mrs Pottage saying, "Oh, no, Paul, what *have* you done?"

"Oh, no!" said Pat.

There was a jumbled pile of letters next to Paul, and he had a letter in his mouth.

"I think he's trying to sort your letters," said Mrs Pottage. "Oh, I am sorry, Pat. What a jumble! Don't worry. We'll all help to sort them out for you."

Mrs Pottage put Paul in his high chair.

"There," she said. "That'll keep him out of mischief."

They spread the letters out on the carpet, making a pile for each person in Greendale. They had nearly finished, when Katy said, "Oh, *look!*"

At the bottom of the heap of letters was a little pile of torn-up paper.

"He's torn up a letter," said Mrs Pottage. "Oh dear. I wonder if it's an important one."

"We can fit it together," said Katy.

"Like a jig-saw puzzle," said Tom.

"Don't worry, Pat," said Katy. "We're good at jig-saws. We'll do it in a jiffy."

Mrs Pottage gathered all the pieces carefully, and put them on the table. They all gathered round and began to sort out the torn pieces of letter.

"It says something about coming on a visit, here," said Tom.

"You're not supposed to read other people's letters," said Mrs Pottage.

"We can't sort it out without reading it," said Katy. "What does this bit say, mum?"

"Hm, can't make it out. Something about a pig, I think. But never mind what it says. Just fit the bits together. I wonder who it's for? They're not going to be very pleased to get their letter in tiny pieces."

They were getting on quite well, when Peter Fogg called. A puff of wind came in with him, and mixed all the pieces up again, so he stayed to help.

Then Granny Dryden popped in and said, "I'll give you a hand if I can only find my glasses."

She emptied her handbag out on the table to try and find them, and some of the pieces of letter got mixed up with handbag things.

"If that letter's for me," she said, you'll have to read it for me. I'd never be able to see it without my glasses."

The Reverend Timms came with the
Parish Magazine, and he stayed to help.

"The Lord will guide us," he said. "I
wonder if it's for me? It could be from my
sister in Australia."

Then he spotted Mrs Pottage's new
library books, and sat down to read one of
them. He wasn't much help after that.

Miss Hubbard called in with a bottle of rhubarb wine. When she saw what they were doing, she said, "Goodness me, you're doing it all wrong. Look here, I'll show you how to do it; you want to put them like this..."

Someone jogged her elbow, and the pieces got all mixed up again. She was so cross that she had to sit down with a cup of tea.

Then baby Paul began to cry, and Mrs Pottage had to pick him up and nurse him till he went to sleep, so she couldn't help with the letter.

There were so many people in that kitchen now, some helping and some not, that they were getting in each other's way. The letter still wasn't sorted out.

Sam Waldron came in with a big box of groceries.

"Where shall I put this?" he said. "Hello, are you playing a game? Who's winning? Ooh, excuse me, this is heavy, I'll have to put it down."

And he put the box on the table, with quite a few pieces of letter under it. When he moved the box quite a lot of small leaves, bits of onion-skin, and squashed peas, had joined the pieces of letter to be sorted.

There was another knock at the door.

"Now who can that be?" said Mrs Pottage. "We'll have all Greendale here, soon."

It was Dorothy Thompson.

"Good morning," she said, "I've brought you two jars of my lemon cheese. I just made it yesterday. It's delicious. You must try it. It's lovely on toast."

Now more tea had to be made, and lots and lots of toast, so that everyone could try the lemon cheese. It was delicious. Now they all had sticky fingers. When they wanted to put a piece of letter down in the place where it just fitted, they found that they couldn't. They had to shake their hands to get the paper off, and then it flew just anywhere.

"I think we'd better all go and wash our hands," said Mrs Pottage. "We'll never do it whilst we're all sticky."

So then they all had to wait their turn at the sink, or in the bathroom, to get unstickied.

Whilst they were in the bathroom, Katy and Tom thought they would like to sail their boats in the bath, so they didn't do any more sorting after that.

Then came another knock at the door.

It was Ted Glen, with the grandfather clock. Mrs Pottage had been waiting years for Ted to mend that clock so she certainly wasn't going to ask him to come another day with it. It might be years and years before he brought it again. Everyone had to move to make room for the clock to be carried in, it was so big.

Even the table had to be lifted out of the way. It was then that it tipped right over, and spilt all the pieces of letter on the floor!

"What's all that paper on the floor?" said Ted.

"That," said Pat, "is one of my letters. We've been trying half the morning to get it fitted together."

"Oh, no it's not!" cried Mrs Pottage.
"Well, it is, but it's my letter as well.
Look! I saw this when we moved the table.
I know the writing. It was his Gran's letter
that Paul tore up."

"What you need now," said Ted, "is a spot of glue, and a nice piece of card. Here, the lid of this grocery box will do. Then, if you spread some glue on the card, like this, you can stick the pieces of letter down as you find them. That way, they'll not keep blowing away, or sticking to fingers, or whatever."

"Ted," said Pat, "you're a genius."

They soon had the letter pieced together, and now Mrs Pottage could read it at last.

"Oh!" she said. "Gran's coming to tea tomorrow, and bringing Auntie Kate, Auntie Pamela and Great Aunt Sylvia.

Gracious me, I haven't seen all the aunts at once for years and years. I'll have to make a cake, and scones, and biscuits. I'm sorry folks! I'll have to speed you on your way. Can't have a kitchen full of visitors when I'm baking."

"And I'll have to be on my way with all these letters," said Pat. "It's a good thing there's only one letter like that."

"I'm glad it was mine that he tore up," said Mrs Pottage, "but I'm sorry we have made you so late, Pat."

"I'll manage," said Pat. "I always do. Whatever happens, the Greendale folk will understand."

One by one, they all went on their way, leaving Mrs Pottage to get her kitchen to rights, and make a start on the baking.

The next day, Mrs Pottage called round at Pat's house. She brought a big tin of cakes, and scones, and home-made biscuits.

"This is just to make up for all that trouble you had with the letters," she said.

"Delicious," said Pat. "Thank you very much."

Pat, and Sara, and young Julian, had a real feast with that tin of good things. It lasted for days.

"I'll tell you what," said Sara. "Next time my mum sends a letter, I'll save it. Then you can drop it near Paul. You never know. He might tear it up."